Enid Blyton

The Caravan Family

Also available in the *Family* series by Enid Blyton

The Buttercup Farm Family

The Queen Elizabeth Family

The Pole Star Family

The Saucy Jane Family

The Seaside Family

Also by Enid Blyton

Amelia Jane Again!

Amelia Jane Gets Into Trouble!

Naughty Amelia Jane!

Amelia Jane is Naughty Again!

Five O'Clock Tales

Six O'Clock Tales

Seven O'Clock Tales

Eight O'Clock Tales

The Adventures of the Wishing Chair

The Wishing-Chair Again

The Magic Faraway Tree

The Folk of the Faraway Tree

The Enchanted Wood

The *Malory Towers* series

The *Mystery* series

The *St Clare's* series

Enid Blyton

The Caravan Family

Mammoth

First published in Great Britain 1945
by Lutterworth Press

Published 1997 by Mammoth, an imprint of Reed International Books Ltd
Michelin House, 81 Fulham Road, London SW3 6RB
and Auckland and Melbourne

Text illustrations by Ruth Gervis
Cover illustration by Richard Jones.

ISBN 0 7497 2856 6
10 9 8 7 6 5 4 3 2 1

A CIP catalogue record for this title
is available from the British Library.

Printed and bound in Great Britain
by Cox & Wyman Ltd. Reading, Berkshire

CONTENTS

1	Round the next corner	7
2	The two caravans	14
3	Moving-in day	21
4	Settling in	28
5	Going to bed in the caravan	36
6	Trouble in the night	42
7	Davey and Clopper	49
8	Off to Uncle Ned's	57
9	A lovely time in the hay	64
10	Learning to milk	71
11	A great time in the dairy	79
12	A wonderful surprise	86

1 ROUND THE NEXT CORNER

DADDY had been away for two long years, and now he was back again! Mummy smiled all day long, and the three children were happy too.

Soon Daddy and Mummy began to talk about where they were going to live. "We can't live with Granny any more," said Daddy. "We must have a home of our own."

"A dear little house in the country!" said Mike, the eldest.

"Called Cherry Cottage," said Belinda, who was next.

"And let's keep cows," said Ann, the youngest.

"We'll try and find all you want," said Daddy, and he laughed.

So they tried. They heard of cottages here and houses there, but oh dear, when they went to see them, they didn't like them a bit!

"Well, whatever are we to do?" said Mummy. "We really can't all live at Granny's for the rest of our lives!"

Then they found one dear little cottage with roses growing all the way up the walls. It was set on a hill and had a lovely view.

"We'll have this!" said Mummy. But the price was very high, and Daddy hadn't enough money to buy it. So that was no good either.

They came away from the cottage feeling rather sad. "We shall never find a home," said Mummy, and she looked so miserable that Daddy put his arm round her and gave her a hug.

"Don't give up hope!" he said. "Why, you may find a home round the very next corner!"

"Things like that don't happen, Daddy," said Mummy, but she laughed.

"I wonder what's round the next corner," said Belinda. "It would be funny if Daddy's words came true!"

"We'll see what houses there are when we come to the next corner," said Mike. So they all looked hard when they came to it.

There were no houses to be seen at all—only

two old caravans, set in the corner of the field !

"They're empty," said Mike. "Can I get over the gate and have a look at them, Daddy ? I've never seen a caravan really close to."

The three children climbed over the gate, while Mummy and Daddy leaned against it, waiting. Ann was the first at the caravans. "There are steps to go up into them," she cried. "Shall we go up ? There's no one here!"

They peeped through a window.

But the doors were locked. The children couldn't get inside. They stood on one of the wheels and peeped through a window.

"They're quite big inside!" said Belinda. "Look!— that's where the stove is—and the smoke comes out of the little chimney-thing at the top. It's awfully dirty inside, though."

The children had a good look at the two caravans. They had once been painted a gay yellow and blue, but now the paint was dull and cracked. The shafts into which horses had once been backed, to pull the caravans along, slanted to the ground, and there were no horses to be seen.

"How I wish *we* lived in a caravan!" said Ann, longingly. "Just think of it, Mike! When we got tired of living in one place, we could put in the horses and go off to another!"

"A house on wheels!" said Belinda. "Mike—why *shouldn't* we live in a caravan? After all—we can't get a house!"

"Let's go and ask Daddy!" said Mike, and the three of them sped off to the gate.

"Daddy! Daddy! Why can't we live in a caravan?" cried Belinda. "Why can't we? Do you suppose these would be for sale?"

Daddy and Mummy laughed. "Live in a

caravan! Oh no, darling, we couldn't do that."

"But why not?" said Ann. "I can think of all sorts of good reasons why we should, and not a single reason why we shouldn't!"

"Couldn't we live in a caravan for the summer—just till we find a house?" said Mike, suddenly. "It would be a kind of holiday, Mummy—and you did say you'd like to go off for a holiday, a long one, now Daddy is home again."

"Well," said Mummy and Daddy together, and looked at one another. A holiday—in caravans

"But why not?" said Ann.

—just till they could find a house ? It wasn't a bad idea at all!

A big burly man came walking along the lane. Daddy spoke to him. "Good afternoon! Could you tell us if these caravans are for sale?"

"They are," said the farmer. "They belong to me. I bought them off some gipsies last year. Why, do you want them ? You can have them cheap."

Suddenly everyone felt very excited. The caravans were for sale—cheap! Oh Daddy, Daddy, do buy them, thought all the children, looking at him with big eyes.

"Well—I'll come along and talk to you about them," said Daddy. And he went along with the farmer.

Will you believe it?— when he came back, he had bought both the caravans! The children hung on to his arms, laughing and shouting in excitement.

"Oh Daddy! They're ours, they're really ours! When can we move in? Oh, our new home *was* just round the corner after all!"

"The caravans will have to be well cleaned, repaired and repainted," said

Daddy. "That will take three weeks. And we must buy two horses. My goodness—we're going to have some fun!"

"We shall be the Caravan Family!" said Belinda. "What adventures we shall have!"

GRANNY held up her hands in horror when she heard that Daddy had bought two caravans.

"My *dear!*" she said, "what *can* you be thinking of? Don't do a thing like that. You can stay with me for always."

"No, Granny dear," said Mummy. "You have had enough of three noisy children in your little house. You deserve a little peace and quiet now. We shall be very happy in the caravans."

Of course, Granny had to go and see them. She thought they were dreadful. "You'll live like gypsies." She said. "I can't bear it."

"Come inside and

have a look," said Belinda, slipping her hand into Granny's. Daddy had the keys now, so the caravans could be unlocked. Granny and Belinda went up the steps to the door of the caravan. It was a funny door. You could open all of it at once if you wanted to—or you could open just the top half and leave the bottom half shut.

"Isn't it a good idea?" said Belinda to Granny. "None of *your* doors open like that, Granny. Now see what a lot of room there is inside this caravan. This will be Mummy's and Daddy's."

Granny looked round. She saw what looked like a big wide room, with

"Come inside and have a look."

two little windows at the front, and a bigger window down each side. There were no curtains, of course. There was an old stove at one end and a very old and dirty sink, with taps.

"Good gracious!" said Granny. "You can even have running water. I didn't know that—and cook too. Well, well, well—it really might be rather exciting."

"Daddy is having two bunks made on this side just like a ship has," said Belinda. "One, the lower one, can be used as a couch in the day-time, and the other will fold down flat against the wall, and be out of the way."

Granny began to get excited. "It *could* be made very nice," she said, "yes, very nice. You can have cupboards or lockers built against the walls to keep your things in. Pretty curtains at the windows. A flap-table built against the wall, that lets down flat when you don't want it. Gay rungs on the floor— and thick cork carpet underneath to keep out the cold and damp."

"All this sounds as if it would cost rather a lot of money," said Mummy, coming in too.

"I shall help you," said Granny, at once. "I didn't like this caravan idea—but if you are set on it, we'll do everything as nicely as possible. I shall help you!"

Well, of course, that made things more exciting than ever, for Granny's ideas of helping were very generous. She took the children shopping with her, and they chose gay blue and yellow rugs for their caravan floor, and a very gay piece of stuff for curtains. Granny got them blue and yellow blankets for their bunks and a blue eiderdown each.

"I'm simply LONGING to live in our caravan!" said Mike, hopping about. "I can't wait. Three weeks is a terribly long time."

It was. But there was a great deal to do. Two men arrived one day to repair the caravans. They put a new wheel on one. They mended the chimney of the other. They took out the old stoves ready for new ones to be put in. They mended the rotten old floorboards.

"Everything is all right now, sir," they said to Daddy. "We can get on with the cleaning and painting."

Then what a to-do there was, cleaning the caravans. They were scrubbed well, even the wheels. Then they were ready for the painting.

"What colours shall we have ?" said Daddy.

"Red," said Mike.

"Green," said Belinda.

"Blue, yellow, orange and white," said Ann.

"Silly!" said Mike. "Mummy, what do *you* want?"

"Let's have yellow and red," said Mummy. "Yellow for the sun that we hope will shine down on us this summer, and red for the roses it will put into your cheeks."

"Oh yes," said the children. "Red and yellow!"

So red and yellow it was. The men let Mummy choose the colours and she chose a ladybird red, deep and clear. She chose a creamy yellow.

Then the men began the painting. They painted the caravans yellow, with red round the windows, and a red edge to the roof. The chimneys were red and yellow and the spokes and rims of the wheels were painted red. The door was yellow, and the shafts were blue.

"The caravans look lovely, lovely, lovely!" cried Ann. "Oh Daddy, oh Mummy, aren't they the finest homes in the world ?"

"We shall have to live in them before we say that !" said Mummy, laughing. "Now we must have the stoves and sinks put in. They are ready to be done tomorrow."

"I'd like to cook."

Men came the next day, and put a fine little kitchen-range in Mummy's caravan, one that would both cook the meals and heat the caravan. But in the children's caravan was put a closed stove, for heating only. "I'd like to cook," wailed Belinda, but Mummy said no, *she* would be the only one doing the cooking!

"But I'd like to cook the bacon and eggs, and put milk puddings into the oven!" said Belinda. "Oh, Mummy, do let us have a stove that cooks, in our caravan! You always said that I must learn to cook someday!"

"Yes—but not in *your* caravan!" said Mummy. "You can come and help me cook in mine if you want to!"

"They're ready to live in now. When can we move in, Daddy, say when ?" cried Mike.

"Next week," said Daddy.

"Oh, I simply can't wait till then!" cried Ann. But she had to, of course!

3 MOVING-IN DAY

AT last moving-in day came. The children awoke at Granny's very, very early. It was a fine day. That was good. Nobody likes moving on a rainy day.

There was very little for the family to take to the caravans, except trunks of clothes, books and toys, for almost everything was now at the caravans.

Men had laid thick cork carpet of dark red on the wooden boards of each caravan, running it a little way up the walls, to keep out draughts. On top of this were the gay rugs the children had chosen.

"I do love the two little sinks," said Mike, remembering them. "Belinda, did you see the big tank near the roof, where we keep the water? Then when we turn the taps, the water comes out of them just as it does here at Granny's."

"There's a big tank under the caravan too," said Ann. "I saw it. We have to keep that full of water as well, and there's a handle thing we have to work when we want to pump the water up into our roof tank."

"There are three lovely bunks for us in our caravan," said Mike. "I shall have the bottom one because I'm the eldest. You have the middle one, Belinda, because you are the next oldest. And Ann can have the top one."

"Oh, I shall like that," said Ann, pleased. "I can climb right up to it each night. How lovely!"

Daddy hired a car with a trailer to take the little family down to the place where the caravans were. Into the trailer were put the big trunks, and all the odds and ends—a few chairs, one or two stools, Mummy's work-stand, a few pictures, some extra rugs, and things like that. There was a box full of china, too, and cooking things.

Granny waved good-bye. "I'll come and have tea with you next week," she said. "You'll have settled in by then!"

"Good-bye, good-bye!" called the Caravan

family, and the car drove off, the trailer jolting along behind it.

"I'm the happiest person in the world," said Ann, her round face red with joy. "I'm going to live in a house on wheels!"

The children could hardly wait till the car arrived at the caravans. But at last they were there.

And there were the caravans, standing in the

And there were the caravans!

field corner, looking so new and gay, in their coats of red and yellow! The children tumbled out of the car to open the gate, and the car and trailer bumped slowly, over the rough field, and came to a stop near the two caravans.

Daddy gave Mike the keys, and the boy sped off to unlock the doors. There was rather a strong smell of new paint, but that would soon pass off. Mike peeped into the caravans with delight.

How simply lovely they looked—so shining and spotless and gay! Mike's heart jumped with joy. What dear little homes to have !

Belinda looked in too, and gave a gasp of delight.

"Aren't the bunks lovely with their blue and yellow bedding! And look at our sink with its two bright taps! And don't you love the gay rugs on the floor? And oh *look*, Mike!—Daddy has kept his promise and had shelves made for our books. Won't they look lovely arranged there?"

The gay curtains flapped in the wind, as Belinda opened the windows. The sweet summer air came blowing in, and the sound of the whispering trees.

"Come and help, Mike and Belinda!" called Daddy, from the trailer. "Bring in

Unpacking everything was the greatest fun.

some of the chairs. Mummy and I will bring the boxes."

It was the greatest fun in the world, unpacking every thing and finding a place for it in the caravan. There were big cupboards flat and long, in each caravan, set with shelves. Mummy and Belinda arranged the china in one of the cupboards in Mummy's own caravan.

Mike and Belinda arranged their books on the shelves, and put their toys into a locker. Then they helped to unpack clothes and put those neatly into the cupboards too.

"Now," said Mummy, "there is one thing we shall all have to remember, especially Mike, who is so untidy—we *must* remember to put everything away tidily. The rule when you are living in a caravan is that everything has a place, and must be kept there."

"Yes, Mike can't leave his clothes about or they'll be trodden on," said Belinda. "Mummy, we promise to keep our caravan neat and tidy and clean."

"Oh *yes*—we'll shake the mats and polish the cork carpet, and keep the sink clean, and clean the windows too!" said Ann.

"Granny will be very surprised if you turn into such useful, helpful little people!" said Mummy. "She was always saying you didn't do enough for yourselves. Well, now that you have a caravan of your very own, just see what you can do!"

At last all the boxes and trunks were unpacked, the chairs and stools given a place, the toys arranged, and a few vases set about the caravans.

"I'll fill them with flowers," said Ann. "Oh, Mummy, won't it be lovely to sleep in our caravans? I'm really longing for bed-time!"

4 SETTLING IN

THE first meal of the Caravan Family was very exciting. Mummy lighted her little fire, and it burned beautifully. "Mike's job will be to see that we always have plenty of wood to burn," said Mummy. Mike thought that would be fine. Things like that didn't seem like work. They just seemed fun.

Mummy set her kettle on the bright fire to boil. Ann skipped down the caravan steps to see if the smoke was coming out of the little red chimney.

"It is, it is!" she cried. "Come and see ! It does look nice."

The others laughed, but they went to see the smoke coming out of the chimney, all the same. "Now the caravan looks alive!" said Belinda. "It is breathing. The smoke is its breath!"

Mummy sent Ann to the farm to ask for eggs. She came back without them.

"There are big geese there," she said. "They hissed at me."

"Ann can't say 'Bo!' to a goose!" said Mike, and he took his little sister's hand. "Come on, Baby. I'll say 'BO !', like that, very loudly, and the geese will let us go by !"

So, when they came to the geese, who raised their heads on their long necks, and hissed, Mike faced

. . . to see if the smoke was coming out.

them boldly. "BO!" he said. "Let us pass."

And the geese, who would not have hurt them, anyhow, waddled off, cackling. Mike and Ann went to the farmhouse, and the farmer's wife gave them twelve eggs.

"Laid by my nice brown hens !" she said to Ann. "Look—would you like to see a goose egg?"

She showed Ann an enormous egg. "Goodness!" said Ann. "That would do for my breakfast, dinner and tea ! The geese won't hurt me, will they?"

"Bless you, no!" said the farmer's wife. "Their hissing and cackling is their way of talking to you."

"I don't like your cows either," said Ann. "They have sharp horns."

"*They* won't hurt you!" said the farmer's wife. "Cows are your friends."

"I don't think they are, really," said Ann. "They moo at me so loudly."

"Well, big animals have big voices," said the farmer's wife, laughing. "The cows give you your milk and butter and cheese. You come along here one day, and I'll show you how to milk a cow."

"You must learn good country ways."

"I could never do that!" said Ann, feeling quite scared.

"Ah, if you live in the country, you must learn good country ways!" said the farmer's wife. "Now, take your eggs, and tell your mother if she wants any milk tomorrow to let me know."

Mummy boiled the eggs for tea. Belinda cut bread-and-butter. Daddy ran down to the little village to buy a cake.

Mike set a blue tablecloth out on the green grass. White daisies grew all round, their yellow eyes looking at the children.

"This is the nicest meal I have ever had," said Belinda, "and it's the nicest egg I've ever tasted. I wish I could have another."

"Well, you can," said Mummy. "There are plenty. Goodness me, Belinda, I wish Granny could see you eating like this ! She was always so upset because she said you played with your food instead of eating it."

"Well, I'm hungry now," said Belinda. "Perhaps people are hungrier when they live in the country than when they live in a town, Mummy."

After tea, Belinda wanted to wash up. Mummy was surprised. "But you hate washing up," she said. "You were quite a naughty girl at Granny's, trying to get out of jobs like that."

"Well, it's such a nice little sink, and I do want to turn on the caravan taps," said Belinda. "Your fire makes the water hot in the tank, doesn't it, Mummy? I can get hot water *and* cold."

So Belinda washed up, and enjoyed turning on the taps and seeing the water rush out into the bright little sink.

Then they all sat on the caravan steps and enjoyed the evening air. The sun was sinking. The shadows of the trees grew longer and longer. The daisies closed their eyes. A bat flew close by, and Belinda squealed.

"Don't be silly," said Daddy. "It's only a bat. If you live in the country you must learn to like and understand the country creatures, Belinda—yes, even bats and beetles, mice and earwigs !"

"Oh, I never could," said Belinda.

"It's because you don't know enough about them that you are afraid of them," said Daddy. "You will have to learn a lot out here—and it will be very good for you, Belinda !"

Ann suddenly yawned, and Mummy saw her.

"Bed-time !" she said. "Go along, you two girls. Get undressed, clean your teeth, and brush your hair well. Give me a call when you are safely in your bunks. Mike can stay up till you're ready, as he is the eldest."

And, for once in a way, no one made any fuss about going to bed. Ah, going to bed in bunks in a caravan, with the green fields outside, and cows pulling at the grass—that was fun, great fun!

"Hurrah for bed-time!" said Ann, and skipped up the steps like a week-old lamb !

Belinda hurried after her, just as anxious to go to bed as Ann.

"Don't be long!" shouted Mike. "It's so exciting to go to bed in a caravan—I can hardly wait. Don't be long!"

"We shan't be very quick!" called back Belinda. "We're going to enjoy every single minute— aren't we, Ann ?"

5 GOING TO BED IN THE CARAVAN

IT really was fun going to bed in the caravan. The two girls undressed and washed. They cleaned their teeth at the little sink, and then they brushed their hair well.

They had to give their hair one hundred strokes with the brush, because Mummy had said that made it nice and shiny. Then they said their prayers, kneeling down beside Mike's bunk.

"I said a big thank you to God for our lovely caravan," said Ann. "It's funny, I've often prayed to God for lots of little things I wanted, and He didn't give them to me—but the loveliest thing of all that's happened to me, which is having a caravan, I didn't even ask Him for."

"Perhaps the little things you thought you wanted wouldn't have been good for you," said Belinda wisely. "And perhaps living in a caravan *will* be good for you. You may learn to like cows, for instance, and geese."

"And you may learn not to squeal at bats!" Ann answered back. "Well, I don't care how good a caravan will be for me, I'm going to enjoy every minute. Are you ready for bed? You'd better call for Mike."

They cleaned their teeth at the little sink.

"Mike, we're ready!" shouted Belinda, putting her head out of the window.

"I'll come and tuck you up later," called Mummy, as Mike ran to his caravan.

Ann had climbed up into the top bunk. It was simply lovely to lie there, in the funny, narrow little bed, and look out of the window on the opposite side. Ann could see a big red and white cow there.

Belinda was now in the middle bunk, and she pulled the blue and yellow blanket round her. She bounced up and down a little. The bunk was quite springy and comfortable.

Mike didn't take long in getting ready for bed. He was soon in the bottom bunk. All the windows were open, and the curtains blew in the breeze. One of the taps dripped a little and made a plink-ponk sound. A cow moo-ed.

"It's lovely," said Belinda. "So exciting. Hallo, Mummy!—Here we all are, cuddled up in our bunks."

Mummy tucked them up and kissed them. She had to stand on the side of Mike's bunk to get to Ann.

"Don't fall out, darling, will you ?" she said. "You'd get quite a bump if you did."

Mummy shut one of the front windows, because the wind blew straight on to the bunks,

"We'll have to be very careful and tidy, here!"

and she was afraid there was too much draught. But she left the others wide open and did not draw the curtains across, because the children begged her not to.

"I do like looking at the trees waving, and the cows, and the birds that sometimes fly across," said Belinda.

"Who has left the tap dripping ?" said Mummy, hearing the pink-plonk of the drops falling into the sink. "Now that's very silly, isn't it? You know there is only just so much water in the tank—and by the time the morning came the tank would be quite empty, and you would have to fill it again.

A lot of trouble for nothing!"

"Sorry, Mummy," said Mike. "I was the last at the little sink. I can see we'll have to be very careful and tidy here!"

"I wish it was winter-time and we could have fire in our little stove," said Ann.

"Well, I'm going to let my fire out at once," said Mummy. "It makes our caravan too hot. Now, go to sleep, all of you!" But who could go to sleep quickly on their first night in a caravan? Not Mike, Belinda or Ann! They lay and talked.

"I can see a cow chewing the cud," said Mike. "You don't know what that means, do you, Ann? Well, the cow pulls at grass and swallows it—then she brings it back into her mouth, later, and chews it when she wants to."

"I wish I could do that with toffees," said Ann. "They'd last a long time then. There goes a bat! I heard it squeak !"

"You must have sharp ears!" said Mike. "Lots of people can't hear the squeak of a bat, you know. I wish one would come in through the window, then we could see it close to."

Belinda gave a wail. "Don't say things like that!

You know I hate bats."

"That's because you're just silly," said Mike. "They're dear little things, really—like tiny mice with wings."

The children lay for a long time listening to the evening sounds. They heard a man calling to another in the distance. It was the farmer shouting to one of his men.

Then they heard a dog barking. The light slowly faded and darkness began to creep into the caravan.

"Oh listen, do listen!" suddenly said Mike, in a low voice. "What's that singing ? Oh, isn't it marvellous ?"

"It's fairy music!" said Ann, sitting up in delight.

"It's a nightingale!" said Belinda. Mummy put her head in at the caravan door and whispered :

"Are you children asleep ? Can you hear the nightingale—and now there's another ?"

With the loud trilling song of the nightingale in their ears, the children at last fell asleep. "How lucky we are!" was Belinda's last thought. "How lucky we are to have nightingales to sing us to sleep!"

6 TROUBLE IN THE NIGHT

MUMMY and Daddy were asleep in the front caravan. The children were all asleep in theirs. Outside, in the night, the nightingales still sang—not one or two now, but dozens of them.

Belinda dreamt of musical-boxes as she slept. Then suddenly she awoke with a jump.

At first she could not remember where she was. Then she knew. Of course, she was in the caravan! She sat up in her bunk. What could have wakened her?

She heard a strange grunting noise outside, and then something bumped against the caravan and shook it violently. Then there came a harsh rubbing sound.

Belinda was frightened. Whatever could it be? She called softly to Mike.

"Mike! Mike! Wake up! I think there's someone trying to get into our caravan! Oh, Mike, do wake up!"

Mike did wake up, and so did Ann. They sat up in their bunks, and when Ann heard the queer noises, and felt the caravan shaking, she began to cry.

"I want Mummy! What is it? I'm afraid."

"It's all right, Ann," said Mike. "I'll go and see who it is."

Mike was just as afraid as the others, but he knew that a boy must always look after his sisters. So he swung his legs out of his bunk, and was just about to stand up when something banged against the caravan at the front.

"Oh, it's gone round to the front now," wailed Ann. "Oh quick, Belinda, shut the window in case it comes in!"

"I'll peep out of the window and see if I can spot anything," said Mike. "If it's a robber, I'll yell for Mummy and Daddy."

He stuck his head cautiously out of the front window, and drew it back again at once.

"Something breathed hard at me," he said.

"I heard it," said Ann. "Oh, there must be things all round the caravan now—it's being bumped from every side!"

So it was. Bump—thud—bump—biff! Ann clung to the sides of her bunk, and opened her mouth to yell.

Before she could yell an enormous noise boomed into the caravan, and Ann almost fell out of her bunk.

Mike suddenly roared with laughter. "It's all right, girls" he said. "It's the cows!"

"*Cows!*" said Belinda, indignantly. "What are they trying to get into the caravan for?"

"They're not," said Mike. "They're just inquisitive, that's all. I suppose they didn't like to come and peep round when we were all about—but now that it's dark and quiet they've come to see where we've got to."

A cow rubbed itself hard against a corner of the caravan, and it shook a little. Then another cow bumped against it.

"*Well!*" said Ann, crossly. "I do think they are bad cows, coming and waking us up like this. Are they going to bump into our caravan all night?"

"No," said Mike, "because I'm going to chase them away!"

He opened the door of the caravan, slipped down the steps, and met a surprised cow face to face in the starlit darkness.

"Moo!" said the cow, startled, and backed away.

"Now you get away from our caravan, please," said Mike, firmly. "Go along! Yes, and you too. And is that another cow there? Well, get away, all of you, and don't come back again till morning. We want to go to sleep."

The startled cows lumbered off to the other side of the field, where they stood for a long time thinking about Mike and his sudden appearance. Mike went back into the caravan.

"You're very brave," said Ann, in great admiration. "They might have put their horns into you."

"It's only bulls that do that, silly," said Mike, getting into his bunk again. "I say, are you girls hot? Shall I leave the door of the caravan open?"

"Oh *no,*" said Belinda. "Why, the cows might all come walking in !"

So the door was shut, and the children soon fell asleep again. They slept soundly. Belinda awoke first, and lay lazily looking out of the window.

"It's lovely to go to sleep in a caravan!" she thought. "But it is even lovelier to wake up in one!"

She slipped out and opened the door. She sat on the topmost step in her nightie, hugging her knees. A nearby thrush sang to her.

"Ju-dee, Ju-dee, Ju-dee!"

"That's not my name," said Belinda. "My name is Belinda, not Judy."

The cows were all lying down now, chewing the cud. The trees whispered secrets together, standing cheek to cheek. A nearby stream made a gurgling sound. "The world looks so clean and fresh and new," thought Belinda, "and the grass is all silvery with dew. The farm dog is up, and so are the birds—and there's a bee too, flying to find some honey. The bee is our friend too. I must tell Ann that."

She ran to help Mummy.

Someone looked out of the window of the other caravan. It was Mummy. "Hallo, Belinda!" she cried. "Are you enjoying this beautiful morning? Hurry up and dress, and you can help me to cook breakfast!"

Belinda didn't wake the others. She dressed quickly and ran to help Mummy.

Soon a smell of bacon and eggs frying crept over the two caravans.

"Breakfast, lazybones, breakfast!" cried Belinda, looking in at the open door of her caravan, and waking up Mike and Ann with a jump. "Come on, do hurry up. I've been up for simply *ages* !"

"You *might* have woken us up too!" said Mike, as he and Ann scrambled into their clothes. "We don't want to miss a single minute of this caravan holiday."

7 DAVEY AND CLOPPER

THE happy summer days went by. The children grew used to a caravan life, and became as brown as ripe acorns. Mike collected wood every day for his mother's fire, and stacked it neatly under the caravan for her. Belinda and Ann carried water from the farmer's well to pour into the tank under the caravan. Daddy pumped it from there into the roof tank when it was needed.

Mummy went down to the village to shop, and the children often went with her to help carry back the things. Belinda and Ann tidied their caravan every day, cleaned the little sink, and shook the mats.

"You are really good, useful children now," said Mummy, pleased. "And the holiday is doing us all good."

But one day the Caravan Family got a shock. The farmer came to Daddy and said

The children went with her to help carry back the things.

he was sorry, but he would have to take the field they were in for two of his bulls.

"This is the only field with a really strong fencing round it," he said. "One of my bulls is such a bad-tempered fellow I must put him somewhere safe now. So I'm afraid I must ask you to go."

Ann burst into tears. "We can't go, we can't !" she said. "We haven't any horses to take us. And the caravans are too heavy for us to pull ourselves."

"That's all right," said Daddy to the farmer. "I didn't mean to stay here all the summer, anyhow. What's the good of having a house on wheels if you stay in the same place all the time? We want a bit of adventure!"

Ann dried her eyes. That sounded lovely, she thought. "But what about horses, Daddy?" she said.

"I can sell you two," said the farmer. "Or if you don't like what I've got to sell you, you can go to the next farm and look at the horses there. You want strong, quiet horses for caravans."

All the Caravan Family went to look at the horses the farmer had to sell—and they loved them at once!

"This is Davey," said the farmer, patting a strong little horse with a white star on its forehead. "You could let the children ride on him, he's so good."

Mike beamed. He had always longed to ride—and now he would be able to!

"And this is Clopper," said the farmer, patting another horse, dark brown and white. "Not quite so good-tempered as Davey here, but a good horse, and strong."

Daddy knew quite a lot about horses. He made the farmer trot them round and about.

"Davey, I do like you!"

He looked at their teeth. He mounted Davey and rode him round the field.

Then he and the farmer bargained together over the price. Daddy knew what he could afford to pay, and he wouldn't go any higher than that. In the end he got the horses for the money he had, and he and Mike led Davey and Clopper proudly to the caravans.

"Now, we've got two horses of our own!" said Ann, in delight. "Davey I do like you. And Clopper, your big shaggy feet make a noise like your name."

"When are we going?" said Mike, who, now that they had horses, was longing to be gone. "Tomorrow? And where are we going?"

"I don't know where!" said Daddy, laughing. "What do you think, Mummy? Have you any idea where you want to go?"

"Let's go to my brother's farm, the children's Uncle Ned," said Mummy, suddenly. "It's almost haymaking time, and the children will love that. They can help. And may be Davey and Clopper could help too.

They could pull the machine that cuts the grass!"

"Oh Mummy—*do* let's go to Uncle Ned's!" cried the children, who had never been there. "We'll help in the haymaking. We'd love that."

"All right," said Daddy. "We'll go there. It will take us a day and a half, I should think. Now Mike, I want to show you how to groom a horse, then you can help me each night. We must look after Davey and Clopper well, for they are now part of our Caravan Family."

The next day there was great excitement. "No packing up when we move!" said Ann, skipping about as Daddy put Davey between the blue shafts of the first caravan. "No buying tickets! No waiting about for a taxi or train!"

"We just put in the horses and off we go!" said Mike, laughing as he backed Clopper into the shafts of his own caravan.

In about half an hour they were all ready to go. The farmer's wife gave them a present of twelve new-laid eggs and a pound of butter.

Daddy was to drive the first caravan, and Mike was to drive the other. Mike was wild with delight. Daddy had explained the harness and the reins to him, and exactly what to do. Mummy was to sit beside him at first, in case he did anything silly.

"I'm to drive our caravan," he told the girls, proudly, and how they stared!

"I want to, too," said Ann at once, but Mummy said no, not yet anyhow.

Daddy sat in front of his caravan, and Mike climbed on the front of his, with Mummy beside him. Each of the girls put their heads out of the front windows, one each side.

Daddy clicked to Davey, and the little black horse set off over the bumpy field, the caravan jolting behind him.

Then came Mike's caravan, the boy proudly holding the reins. "Clopper could go without you driving him," said Belinda.

"Don't disturb me," said Mike, "or I might drive into a ditch."

"We're off, we're off in our house on wheels!" sang Ann. "We're going far, far away and our house is coming too! Good-bye, cows; good-bye, geese; we're off and away!"

And down the winding lane went the two red and yellow caravans, with Ann singing at the top of her voice.

8 OFF TO UNCLE NED'S

WHAT fun it was to travel for miles and miles in a caravan! Davey and Clopper did not go fast, but they went very steadily.

The countryside was very beautiful just then. Sometimes the children could smell honey suckle on the wayside hedges. They heard the little yellowhammer singing, "Little bit of bread and no *cheese*" as loudly as he could.

The corn was growing well, waving sturdy and green in the wind. Some farmers were already haymaking as the two caravans passed by.

"Oh, I do hope Uncle Ned won't have finished his haymaking by the time we get there," said Belinda, who had set her heart on helping.

Daddy had a map to show him the way to

Uncle's farm. It was fun to look at it with him and see the way.

"By a wood, down a hill, along by this river," said Daddy, reading the map, and pointing with his finger. "Yes, we should be there by tomorrow afternoon."

Down long dusty lanes went the two caravans, the horses' hooves making a clipclopping noise as they walked. Daddy kept off the main roads when he could. The lanes were so much prettier.

Sometimes the girls sat in their caravan, and sometimes they ran beside it. Once there was a great scare because Ann disappeared!

"Ann! Where's Ann?" suddenly said Mummy. "She was running beside the caravan a few minutes ago. Belinda, where's Ann?"

Belinda was now sitting beside her father in the front of the first caravan. "I don't know, Mummy," she said. "Isn't she in the road? That's where I saw her last."

"Oh dear—we must have left her behind somewhere!" said Mummy. "I'll turn this caravan

"Fast asleep under your eiderdown !"

round and go back to find her. You can stay here and give Davey a rest, Daddy."

So Mummy and Mike turned their caravan round and went back to look for the missing Ann. But they couldn't find here anywhere!

They didn't know what to do. Mike felt alarmed. Poor little Ann! She would be so frightened. Had she wandered off and got really lost?

"Well, I don't know what to do," said Mummy, at last. "We've gone back a long way. Oh look—there's Dadddy coming with his Caravan—and how fast Davey is going!"

Daddy shouted out as he came near : "We've got Ann! She was fast asleep curled up under your eiderdown in your bunk!"

Well, Mummy and Mike *did* feel glad. Ann was surprised to find what a fuss everyone suddenly made of her when she sat sleepily in the bunk.

"Well, after that shock, I think we'll draw up on this bit of common, and have a meal and a bit of a rest," said Daddy. "The horses want a drink and a rest, too. Take them to that pond, Mike, and then tether them loosely to some post or tree."

They spent a lazy time over their meal. Davey and Clopper pulled at the grass, and then lay down in the sun. The caravans gleamed gaily in the bright sunshine, and the windows winked and blinked.

"Well—off we go once more," said Daddy. "And mind—if anyone thinks of going to sleep under eiderdowns again, will they please warn us before they do?"

Everyone laughed. Daddy took his place behind Davey, and Mike took his behind Clopper. Mummy went inside her own caravan to wash up the few picnic things. Mike was quite able to drive Clopper by himself now.

That night they camped in a field full of

big moon-daisies and red sorrel. The horses, well-fed, watered and rubbed down, lay contentedly in the shadow of the caravans.

"Last night we were somewhere different, and tomorrow we'll be somewhere else too," said Ann, sleepily. "I do like living in a caravan with horses to take you wherever you want to go."

They set off again the next day, and the children got excited when at last they drew near to Uncle Ned's big farm.

"Won't he be surprised to see us!" they said. "Oh, let's hope he hasn't done his hay-making yet!"

"That's the boundary of Uncle's farm," said Mummy, suddenly, pointing to a wood in the distance. "Now we are nearly there."

They came to a big field, where long grass, clover and buttercups waved together. Two or three men were there, talking. Mummy gave a call.

"Ned! Hi, Ned! Hallo, there! Hallo!"

In the greatest surprise Ned turned—and when he saw the two gay caravans, with Mummy, Daddy, and the three children

"Hallo, there! Hallo!"

waving to him, he could hardly believe his eyes!

"*Well!*" he said at last, and ran to the lane to welcome them all. "*Well!* What a wonderful surprise! Won't your Aunt Clara be astonished? Where did you come from? How long are you staying?"

"As long as you'll have us," said Daddy. "We've come to help with the haymaking. I see you haven't begun yet."

"No, not yet," said Uncle Ned. "I wanted to begin it last week because the weather was so fine, but I've had a bit of bad luck."

"Why, what's wrong?" asked Mummy. "I hope it's nothing serious, Ned!"

"I've two of my horses ill," said Uncle Ned, "so I can't cut the grass yet."

"We'll lend you Davey and Clopper!" cried Mike. "They'll pull the machine for you. They're proper farm-horses, really they are!"

"Come along to the farm-house," said Uncle Ned. "Well, well, this is a bit of good news, to be sure. A whole family to visit me—and two horses to lend me! We'll all start the haymaking tomorrow!"

So off they went to the farm-house, all talking at the top of their voices!

9 A LOVELY TIME IN THE HAY

UNCLE NED and Aunt Clara were simply delighted to welcome the Caravan family. They gave them a glorious tea, and then went to see the two gay caravans.

"This is *my* sleeping-bunk, the topmost of all," said Ann, proudly.

"And look—our taps have running water!" said Mike, and he turned one on. "And in Mummy's caravan there is hot water from one tap, when she has the fire going. I collect the wood for it every day."

"It's all lovely," said Auntie Clara. "I almost wish I lived in a caravan too. So you've come to help with the haymaking, have you? Well, we want all hands then, I can tell you!"

"We'll begin tomorrow," promised Mike. "We will work just as hard as anybody else, because since we've lived so much in the open air, we have all grown strong and healthy."

Next day the fun began. First of all Davey and Clopper were put to drag the grass-cutting machine. They pulled it along, and the knives of the machine cut the grass easily, leaving it behind in big piles.

"How funny the hay-field looks now!" said Ann, dancing among the short stems. "It's had its hair cut! Now can we begin to toss the hay, Uncle?"

"Toss it as much as you like," said the farmer. "The drier it gets, the better I shall like it! Hasn't the hay a lovely sweet smell now?"

The long cut grass turned a grey-green colour and smelt delicious. Belinda said she would like some scent made of it, to put on her hanky.

The children tossed it about, threw it at one another, rolled over and over in it, and had a lovely time. Scamper, the farm dog, came to join them. He was a big collie, and he had a fine time, too.

"He's haymaking as well!" said Ann, and

The children had a lovely time.

tried to bury him in the sweet-smelling hay. But he wouldn't be buried.

Everyone was pleased next day when they were given big hand-rakes and told to turn the rows of hay over, so that the sun could dry the wet bits underneath. The children worked very hard.

The sun shone down hotly, and Uncle Ned was pleased. "Just right for the hay!" he said. "It will dry beautifully, and I shall get it quickly away and built into hay-stacks before the rain comes."

"Then your cows will have lots to eat in the winter, won't they?" said Belinda.

When the hay had been well raked and turned the farmer said it must be got into neat wind-rows—big long rows all the way down the field.

"Fetch Davey," he said to Mike. "Put him in that big horse-rake machine, Mike, then lead him up and down the field. The girls will love to see how the enormous rake at the back of the machine puts the hay into long neat rows."

The girls did like watching, as Mike proudly led the horse-rake up and down the field. "Mike, push the big steel teeth slide under the hay and get hold of it!" cried Belinda.

"Yes," said Mike. "And now see what happens. As soon as the rake is full of hay, I pull at this handle, which lifts up the steel teeth—and then the hay is neatly dropped in a long row. Isn't it clever, Ann ?"

Before the evening came the hay was all collected into wind-rows by the horse-rake, and Mike's legs were quite tired of walking up and down the field.

"Now to build the hay-cocks!" cried Auntie Clara, who was helping. The children liked her very much. She was pretty and jolly, and she had brought them out a really lovely picnic lunch.

The children helped to build the hay-cocks all down the field. How pretty they looked in the evening sun, with their shadows slanting behind them!

"I do think a hay-field looks lovely with its hay-cocks standing so quietly there," said Belinda. "Mike—look, there's Ann, fast asleep in that corner ! Let's bury her in hay !"

So they did, and soon there was nothing to be seen of Ann at all. She was just another hay-cock! Mummy was astonished to see no Ann, and went hunting and calling for the little girl, while Mike and Belinda ran away, giggling.

Ann heard her mother calling, and woke

up. What was this all round her ? What a funny blanket, thought Ann, trying to sit up. She called to her mother.

"Mummy! Mummy! Where am I?"

"Bless the child, she's a hay-cock!" said Mummy, laughing, and picked her out of the hay. "Come along, darling, it's time for supper and bed. You're tired out."

"It's been such fun," said Ann, sleepily. "What

"I do think a hay-field looks lovely."

do we do next with the hay?"

"As soon as I can I shall take it in the big hay-wagon to the rick-yard," said her Uncle. "Some I shall store in my sheds, and what is left I shall build into hay-stacks."

"Can we ride home on the hay-wagons?" asked Mike. "It's such fun to do that. I shall lie on the very, very top of the hay in the wagon, and look up at the sky, and smell the sweetness of the hay."

"You shall do all that and more!" said Mummy. "But come along home to your caravan now—you are almost falling asleep on your feet !"

So back to the caravans they went, and fell asleep at once, with the sweet smell of the hay drifting in at the caravan window. What a lovely time they were having!

10 LEARNING TO MILK

IT was great fun living near Uncle Ned's farm. He told Daddy the best place to put the caravans.

"Go into that field," he said, pointing. "It's not too far from the farm-house, you'll be sheltered from the wind, and there's a clear stream nearby for washing water. Drinking water you can get from the well outside the farm-house."

So the two caravans were placed there, and a very cosy, sunny spot it was. Cows lived in the field, and Davey and Clopper lived there too. They helped Uncle Ned, and he was glad of them.

"They're fine horses for work," he said, fondling their big noses. "When you're tired of caravanning, I'll buy them from you!"

"We shall never, never be tired of living in a caravan!" said Ann. "And I don't want to sell Davey and Clopper. I love them. Davey always gives me a ride when I ask him."

Each morning and evening the cows were taken to the sheds to be milked. The children went to watch, and they loved to hear the splish splash of the milk in the big pails. Mike wanted to try his hand at milking.

"All right, you can try," said Auntie Clara, and she gave him a milking-stool to sit on. "That's right—get close up to the cow. Have you got strong hands? Yes, you have—but you want to be gentle, too, not rough."

Mike began to milk the cow, but he wasn't very good at it. He got some milk, but it took him a long time to get even half a pail full.

"There isn't any nice froth on it like yours, Auntie," he said.

"No," said Aunt Clara. "That's the sign of a good milker, you know—froth on the top. You try, Belinda!"

So Belinda tried, and she was really very good

"All right—you can try !" said Auntie Clara.

indeed ! Her strong little hands worked away, and the swish of the milk in the pail was a pleasant sound to hear. There was plenty of froth too! Belinda felt very proud.

Then Ann wanted to try. "But you're afraid of cows, silly!" said Mike.

"Oh, I'm not now," said Ann, and she wasn't. Living in the country and doing all kinds of jobs had made her much more sensible. She didn't think cows would run after her and toss her now! She sat down on the stool beside a big, gentle cow called Buttercup.

But Ann's hands were too small for milking, and she soon gave it up. "Belinda's the one!" she said. "Mike and I are no good at milking."

"Yes, Belinda is good," said her aunt. "Now Belinda, be sure to get every drop of the last milk from your cow—that is always the richest!"

"Are you going to make butter from the cream you get off the top of the milk?" said Ann. "Can I help you when you do that, Auntie? Do let me!"

"All right, you shall," said Auntie Clara. "I make butter every Friday. You come along to the dairy then, and you shall help me!"

Mike took the cows back to the field when they were milked. One of them opened its mouth to moo, and Mike had a great surprise. He called to his Uncle.

"I say, Uncle—this cow, Buttercup, opened her mouth wide just now—and, do you know, she's lost all her top teeth ! Poor, poor thing—she won't be able to eat !"

Uncle Ned gave a big roar of a laugh. "What things you do say!" he said. "A cow never has any upper teeth, silly boy! Didn't you know *that*?"

Mike went rather red. Ann and Belinda came skipping up to see what Uncle Ned was laughing at. He opened the cow's mouth and made them look into it.

"Do you see what she has instead of upper teeth?" he said. "There's a bare fleshy pad there—no teeth at all. You see, a cow just pulls at the grass and breaks it off—then she swallows it down into one of her four stomachs—"

"*Four* stomachs!" cried the three children together. "*Four!*"

"Well—four stomachs, or one stomach with four rooms in it, whichever you like," said Uncle. "The cow pulls the grass, and swallows it down straight away into stomach

"Do you see what she has instead of upper teeth!"

number one. Then, when she is resting, she brings back the grass again to her mouth, and spends a very happy time chewing it!"

"Yes, I know," said Mike. "That's called chewing the cud, isn't it?"

"Right!" said Uncle. "Then, when the grass is chewed, the cow sends it down to her second stomach, and from there it goes to the third and to the fourth."

"What a funny animal a cow is!" said Belinda. "Not a bit like a horse! A horse has strong upper teeth. Davey has and so has Clopper. Have they got four stomachs too, Uncle?"

"No, only one," said her uncle. "And their hooves are different too. Look at Buttercup's hoof, Mike."

Mike lifted it up, and gave a cry of surprise. "It's split in two! Not a bit like Davey's, who has his hoof quite whole."

"The cow always has a split hoof," said Uncle Ned. "It helps her when she walks on damp ground, as she often does. All right, Buttercup, we've finished with you! Go and join the others!"

Buttercup, surprised at having her mouth

looked at so closely, lumbered away with a moo.

"I like cows now," said Ann. "I used to think they were so fierce—but they are gentle and slow and friendly. I say—won't it be fun to help to make the butter on Friday?"

11 A GREAT TIME IN THE DAIRY

ON the next Friday the children did their caravan jobs quickly, because they all wanted to rush off to the farm and watch butter being made.

They made their beds and tidied their caravans. They cleaned the sink, and pumped up water from the tank beneath the caravan to the roof-tank, so that there would be plenty to run down to the taps when they were turned on.

Mike shot off to collect wood for his mother's fire, and stacked it neatly under the caravan. Belinda and Ann ran down to the village to buy a few things their mother wanted.

"Is that all, Mummy?" said Belinda, when she brought back the things and put them into her mother's cupboard. "Can we go to the dairy now, and watch Auntie Clara ?"

"Off you go!" said Mummy, pleased to

Mike shot off to collect wood.

see the children's rosy-brown faces, and to know how much they were learning of good country ways. They would have to go to school in the autumn—but meanwhile they were learning country lessons they would never, never forget.

The children rushed to the dairy as fast as they could go, hoping that Auntie Clara hadn't begun her butter-making without them. Ann's legs weren't as long as the others' so Mike waited for her.

Belinda got to the dairy first. She looked round the big, cool, white-washed placed, with its stone floors and shelves. It was lovely!

"Auntie! Oh Auntie, you've begun to make the butter!" she cried in dismay. But her aunt shook her head with a smile.

"Oh no, I haven't. This isn't the butter-churn I'm using. This is the milk and cream separator I'm working—it separates the milk from the cream for me. Then I can use the cream for my butter."

Ann and Mike came in, and they watched with Belinda, as their aunt turned the handle of the separating-machine. "Watch the two pipes that come out there from the side of the machine," said Auntie Clara.

The children watched. They had seen their aunt pour fresh milk in at the top of the separator—and now, lo and behold, out of the two side-pipes came milk and cream, quite separate!

"The top pipe has got cream coming out of it!" said Belinda. "And the bottom pipe has milk. Oh Auntie, isn't it clever?"

"Can I turn the handle, please?" asked Ann. "Do let me!" So Ann turned the handle, and was delighted to see the milk and cream flowing separately out of the two pipes.

The cream was added to some cream already in a great big crock. "Now for the butter," said Auntie Clara, rolling up her sleeves. "That always makes me hot. The butter-churn isn't so easy to use as the separator!"

The butter-churn was a big beech-barrel mounted on a wooden frame. It had a handle too. Auntie Clara poured the cream into the churn. It did look thick and yellow and delicious. Ann poked her finger into it and got it covered with cream, which she licked off.

"Naughty!" said her aunt. "You're as bad as the

farm cat. She's always hanging round taking a lick at the milk-pails and a lick at the cream-crock!"

She took hold of the handle and began to turn it. To the children's surprise the whole barrel turned over and over.

"Oh, hark at the cream, splashing away inside!" cried Belinda. "What a lovely sound!"

"Auntie, how does the churn make butter ?" asked Ann, puzzled.

"Cream goes solid when it's whipped, or when its shaken about like this," said Auntie Clara, her face getting red, for the churn

"You're as bad as the cat!"

was heavy. "It's being shaken about well inside this churn—the butter will soon come."

"I want to turn it," said Ann, but it was too heavy for her. It was too heavy for Belinda too, but Mike's strong arms turned it quite well.

"Ah—the butter's coming!" said Auntie Clara, when she took the handle again. "I always reckon it takes about twenty minutes. Some folks take longer—butter comes quickly for me, thank goodness!"

Their aunt took the lid off the churn and let the children look inside. Where was the thick cream? It was gone! Instead they saw lumps of yellow butter swimming in what looked like thin milk.

"That's the buttermilk," said their aunt, putting the lid on. "Now—just a minute or two more and the butter will be ready!"

She swung the churn over and over again, and then stopped. The lumps of butter were taken out and washed. Then with a wooden butter-roller clever Aunt Clara made the butter firm and hard.

"Let me help you make it into half-pound and pound pats!" cried Mike, who was clever with his hands. Soon the shelf was piled with the neat butter-pats, all wrapped up in the printed farm paper.

"Auntie Clara, I'd like to help you to make the butter each week, and separate the milk and cream too," said Mike suddenly. "Belinda is helping to milk the cows each day, and Ann says she wants to help to feed the hens. So I'll help with the butter. I'm strong, and I can easily swing the churn."

"Thank you, Mike," said his aunt, gratefully. "There's so much to do on a farm just now—I'd be glad to have your help."

"We *love* helping!" said Ann.

"In return for helping to milk the cows, I shall give Belinda four pints of milk a day," said Auntie Clara. "And for helping me with the butter, you shall have two pounds of it each week, Mike—and for helping with the hens you shall have two dozen eggs, Ann!"

Well, wasn't that simply lovely!

12 A WONDERFUL SURPRISE

THE summer days went by far too quickly. "Oh dear!" sighed Mike. "I wish these lovely exciting days wouldn't fly so fast!"

"Well, we've done a tremendous lot of things since we became a Caravan Family," said Belinda. "And I've made up my mind about one thing— and that is that I will always live in the country if I can. It's much nicer than a town."

"Yes—real, proper things happen in the country," said Mike. "Things grow—and calves and lambs are born—and hay is cut—and sheep are sheared—and cows are milked —and—"

"And the harvest is brought in!" said Ann, remembering how she had helped with that. "Oh, weren't the fields of corn lovely, Mike, when they were tall and golden and ripe?"

"I liked watching that wonderful self-binding machine at work in the fields," said Mike. It certainly had been amazing to watch. It had cut the corn, gathered it into sheaves, tied each sheaf neatly with string, and then had thrown the sheaf on to the ground!

"Harvest-home was fun," said Belinda. "I liked going with the wagons to the rick-yards—and wasn't the harvest-home supper grand fun, Mike?"

Everyone, from the oldest farm worker, Tom, to little Ann, had sat down to a grand supper given by Auntie Clara, when the last wagon of corn had been taken to the yard, ready for corn-stacks to be built later on. Ann had fallen fast asleep in the middle of the feast.

But now those lovely days were past, and September was in. Blackberries were beginning to ripen on the hedges, and Mummy had already made a blackberry tart.

Mike's heart was sad. He knew that he and Ann and Belinda were soon to go to school again. They

Blackberries were beginning to ripen.

had already missed a whole term. They could not do that any more.

"Now I suppose we'll have to go and live in a house," he groaned to the girls, as they sat on the steps of their caravan, waiting for Mummy and Daddy to come back from the station.

"Mummy might not have found a school that would do for us," said Belinda hopefully. "Perhaps we shall live in our caravan all the winter."

"I can't bear to think we'll have to say good-bye to Davey and Clopper," said Ann, looking ready to cry. "I do love them so."

"There's the smoke from the train," said Belinda. "Mummy and Daddy will soon be here. Let's go over the fields and meet them."

So the three little caravanners, all as brown as berries, hurried off to meet their mother and father.

"There they are!" said Ann, and waved. Two people, coming over a field, waved back. Mike rushed ahead to meet them.

"Did you find a school? Say you didn't! Say we can still live in our caravan and not in a house!" Mike almost shouted his questions.

"We'll tell you when we get to the caravans," said Mummy. "Have you got the kettle boiling for tea, Belinda, as I asked you ?"

Belinda nodded. "Yes, Mummy—and the bread and butter is cut—and there's a fresh lettuce or two—and some of Auntie's strawberry jam, and a chocolate cake she made for us."

"Good!" said Daddy, and looked forward to such a nice tea, eaten sitting on the soft grass, with cows nearby, and Davey and Clopper nosing up for tit-bits.

"Well," said Mummy, when they were seated at their picnic tea, "well—we've found a school, a fine one too, that teaches gardening and riding and swimming and allows you to keep pets, and has cows to milk and pigs and goats and hens!"

The children cheered up a little. "And no proper lessons at all?" said Ann, hopefully.

"Of course there will be lessons !" said Daddy. "You must learn how to use your brains, or they won't be any use to you or to other people."

"When do we go?" said Belinda, gloomily.

"The school begins next week," said Mummy.

The children looked gloomier and gloomier. Only a few days more, and they would have to say good-bye to Davey and Clopper and the two gay caravans.

"But Mummy and I have decided that we will live near the school in our caravans," said Daddy, smiling. "And we have arranged that you shall be school children all the week—and caravan children from Friday to Monday! How will that suit you?"

"Oh ! OH!" yelled the children, and got up and danced round in delight. "Can we really live in our caravan every week-end? All the winter too? Aren't we going to have a house after all? Shall we still be the Caravan Family?"

"Yes," said Mummy and Daddy, laughing at the children's surprise and joy. "And we had better set off tomorrow in the caravans, because it will take two or three days to get to the school, and we want to be well settled in before you start."

"Davey! Clopper! Do you hear?" called Ann, running to the two horses, who lifted their heads to listen to her. "We're going travelling again tomorrow with you! Oh, won't it be fun?"

So, the next day, they said good-bye to Auntie Clara and Uncle Ned, and thanked them for a lovely time. They put Davey and Clopper between the shafts, and Daddy and Mike took the reins.

"Shall we still be the Caravan Family?"

Then off they went, rumbling over the field to the gate.

"The Caravan Family is off again!" cried Ann. "Our wheels are turning fast, and soon we shall be miles away. Good-bye, good-bye!"

Good-bye little Caravan Family. We hope you'll have lots more fun!

Also available in this series

The Seaside Family

The Caravan Family are spending their summer in beautiful, sandy Sea-gull Cove. They are staying in their caravans, right at the edge of the sea, and it promises to be the best holiday ever! But poor, miserable Benjy John is with them. Will he ruin the children's holiday, or can they cheer Benjy up and help him enjoy the sea and life in a caravan . . . ?